Arthur Tracy Lee

Army Ballads

And other Poems

Arthur Tracy Lee

Army Ballads
And other Poems

ISBN/EAN: 9783744784351

Printed in Europe, USA, Canada, Australia, Japan

Cover: Foto ©Andreas Hilbeck / pixelio.de

More available books at **www.hansebooks.com**

ARMY BALLADS,

AND

OTHER POEMS.

BY

ARTHUR T. LEE, U. S. A.

WITH ILLUSTRATIONS DESIGNED BY THE AUTHOR

1871.

CONTENTS.

OH! THE MOON IS SHINING DOWN.

Oh! the moon is shining down
On our snowy canvas town,
And the rivulet runs laughing to the sea, my love ;
But my heart is sad and low,
For I think of long ago,
When the rivulet but laughed for thee and me, my love.

'Twas the autumn of the year,
And the leaf was red and sear,
But our hopes were bright as springtime's budding
bough, my love,
They blossomed, but they died,
Fell and drifted with the tide,
To the ocean where our joys are buried now, my love.

Dost thou ever think of me,
By that river of the sea,
Where the breath of hawthorn blossoms filled the
plain, my love,
When the glowworm lit the shade,
Whilst our vows of love were made,
To be broken ere the blossoms came again, my love ?

They tell me thou art gay,
In thy palace far away,
Where another gains the smiles that once were mine,
    my love,
And my heart is sad and low,
For I think of long ago,
And the folly of this heart that once was thine, my
    love.

Whilst the moon is shining down
On our snowy canvas town,
And the rivulet runs laughing to the sea, my love,
Here I cast upon the stream,
All remembrance of the dream,
That is laughing water now to thee and me, my love.

THE DRUMMER BOY.

Ay !—rattle away, with a heart full of joy,
And a lip full of sweetness, thou merry eyed boy;
The pride of thy bosom there's naught can subdue,
As it swells 'neath its jacket of crimson and blue.

When morn from the east flings her earliest beams,
Thou art first with thy young arm to banish our
    dreams,
And the eye of the sternest falls softly on thee,
As thou roll'st the long roll of the loud reveillé.

They say thou wert born in the camp, when the flash
Of battle gleamed red on each tent,—and the clash
Of arms,—and the groan, and the scream of the fight,
Was the music that welcomed thy spirit to light.

They sought for thy father, at dawning of morn,
But thy mother was husbandless when thou wert born.
He gave up his life that his child might be free,
And left but his glory, to mantle o'er thee.

11

I heard thee but yesterday boastingly tell,
How strong was his arm,—and how bravely he fell;
And thy delicate fingers grew white as they played
Convulsed o'er the hilt of thy glittering blade.

Thou look'st to the world but a drummer boy, now,
Yet time will toss back those bright locks from thy
    brow,
And light in thy dark eye ambition's wild flame,
The torch of the soldier who strikes for a name.

I look on the fields that are yet to be won,
Where the smoke of artillery darkens the sun;
There thy brow wears the white plume, the pompon is
    gone,
And thy voice gives the word as the column moves on.

Then rattle away, with a heart full of joy,—
And a lip full of sweetness, thou merry eyed boy;—
In the gathering tide of thy fate there's a wave,
That may lift thee as high as the best of the brave.

'THE EXPRESS RIDER.

Come forth,—day is breaking, my gallant steed,
Come forth,—'tis a day that must try thy speed;
I have far, far to ride through the hammocks green
Where in ambush the red savage lies unseen.
Nor bramble, nor drift sand must stay thy flight,
For my lash is keen, and my spur is bright;
And well dost thou know how the thong is played,
When the sharp shot rings in the cypress shade;
When I twist my hand in thy flowing mane,
No need then to pull on the foamy rein;
And the tall palmetto, and mangrove drear,
We leave behind in our swift career,
As with lightning limb o'er the sands ye fly,
For the open plain, and the open sky.

  Oh! the music, no heart loves like my own,
Of thy clashing hoof in the forest lone;
It frights the dark wolf from his lazy pace,
It starts the red deer from his hiding place,
It drowns the wild whoop when the danger is past
²And the tall pine's shadow is over us cast.

13

³When thy wild eye tells me the foe is near,
And the wild yell breaks on my startled ear,
Then I trust to thy speed,—and the hand to save
Of Him who keeps watch o'er the true and brave!
   'Tis mine, to scatter the seeds of care,
In the hearts and homes of the young and fair;
And I ofttimes think, as I onward go,
Of the sources I carry of joy and wo;
Glad hopes for the maiden whose heart is bound,
To the soldier whose couch is the tented ground;
To the sister who blends with a brother's name,
The honored meed, and the gilded fame;
But tidings, oh! sad, for the mother's ear,—
A son hath been borne, on a lowly bier,
To an early grave in the wild-wood dim,
Where the night bird croaks on the cypress limb.
   Of thousands, I carry the joys and fears;
Though I never shall see their smiles or tears.
I halt my steed at the fortress gate—
Ah! what anxious faces around me wait;
The gay youth grasps, with an eager hand,
The lines from his love in a far off land;
Whilst a father looks on the sable seal,
With a wound in his heart that no hope can heal;
His manly limbs as with ague shake
And the warning seal he dares not break,—

'

One single sentence may bring despair ;
His wife, his sons, and his daughters fair,
He sees them all as he saw them last,
Yet knows that one from the earth has passed ;
And he dares not learn which hope is dead ;
Whose claim are the tears he so soon must shed.

   And yet, to this life do I joyous cling ;
For I'm welcome, whate'er be the news I bring ;
And I love,—oh! I love, when the full moon shines,
To fly, 'neath the shade of the dark, tall pines,
When the south-wind that plays with my flowing hair,
Is not half so light as the heart I bear.
And then there is somebody, fair and bright ;
Who watches for me, in the pale moon's light ;
When the tramp of my steed in the dark pass rings,
And is borne to her ear, on the night wind's wings ;
To know that her glad tears are falling fast,
Is reward enough for the dangers past.

   Oh! a life like mine,—who'd lay it down,
For the idle pomp of the painted town ?
Not I,—not I,—for I love too well,
In the heart of the forest green to dwell ;
And I heed not the gay world, whate'er it be ;
For the wild-wood is world enough for me.

LIGHT ON THE WAVE.

SONG.

Light on the wave!—the moon shines bright!
　Pass the bowl,—fling sorrow away, my boys!
The breeze is fair,—we will rock to-night,
　On the wave of Aransas Bay, my boys!

We have slept in the calm,—we have laughed in the
　　gale,
　We have sung by the pale moon's light, my boys!
But by morning's dawn, should the breeze not fail,
　We'll bid to the sea, good night, my boys!

Light hearts we bring to this stranger land;
　Though a shadow hath hung o'er them late, my
　　boys!
And we drain our cups, with a steady hand;
　And a smile for whate'er be our fate, my boys!

We will some of us sleep 'neath the prairie sod,
　We will some go back o'er the sea, my boys!
But the hearts that are true to their country and God
　Will all meet at the last reveillé, my boys!

16

Then pass 'round the bowl!—the moon shines bright!

   Our wild campaign began, my boys!

We bid to the sea, a glad good night!

   And to-morrow will fight, if we can, my boys!

WHEN SOFT AND LOW.

When soft and low,—when soft and low,
O'er the prairies wild the west-winds blow,
I loose my heart, and it flies to thee,
O'er a thousand miles of land and sea;
Softly it steals to thy place of rest;
To dwell 'till dawn on thy snowy breast;
And steal from thine eye, the dream wrought tear,
To moisten mine whilst I slumber here.

If sorrow creeps to my heart by day,
To darken its wild hopes, far away,
The scenes of home, that my dreams adorn,
Bring gladness back with the dawn of morn :
Then I hail the sun, at the bugle's clang,
And fling myself on my dark mustang;
With a heart as light, and a joy as wild
As the flying foot of a mountain child.

I've a priceless jewel, far away,
Though I cannot recall its look to-day ;
I know that its eyes like its mother's are,
When she wears the look that she used to wear;

And I love that **child of** my midnight dreams,
For the mother's blood that through it streams;
God spare that heart! **that** it long may throw
Hope's buds on mine, when the west **winds** blow.

PAT'S LAMENT.

Och! I'm sick of this war of all talk and no fighting,
  Ten years have I served in the Infantry corps;
And I've not made my mark yet, to show my hand-
        writing;
  On Indian behind, or on Aztec before.
It's burnish, and pipe-clay, and stand for inspection.
Och! blood,—I'd as soon be laid out for dissection:
    It's "mind your toes! turn them out!"
    All the day, "cast about!"
  Not a corporal yet, and I shan't be, what's more.

For thirteen long months did I serve in the everglade,
  Neck deep in debt, and full waist deep in mud:
O'er dirty lagoon, and through streams I could never
        wade:
  Batt'ling it bravely, but spilling no blood.
My limbs are rheumatic, I have not a dollar now;
My hair has grown gray, but I scarce know its color
        now:
    For my captain so very sleek,
    Has me cropped every week,
  And the least show of whisker he "nips in the bud."

From the " Land of bright flowers," I've now crossed
      the ocean,
  With twenty-four buck and ball rounds in my box ;
And an old aching heart that cries loud for promotion,
  And ne'er murmured yet, at hard bread or hard
      knocks.
But alas ! for my hopes, I find now they associate
Blood, war and death, with the soft word, *negotiate.*
     Head crop'd, and whisker lop'd ;
     Grog stop'd,—promotion drop'd :
  'Tis enough to dishearten the soul of an ox !

DOWN IN SWEET WYOMING VALE.

Down in sweet Wyoming vale,
With a maiden sad and pale,
I wandered in the rosy month of June;
When the clover blossom rare,
Scented all the summer air;
As it floated 'tween the valley and the moon.

Down in sweet Wyoming vale,
When the autumn leaves did pale,
And the clover blossom kissed the breeze no more—
Where bright Susquehanna flows,
There I plucked a faded rose,
From a lowly mound that sleeps beside the shore.

Down in sad Wyoming vale,
Now the wild November gale
Comes with wailing through the forest brown and sear,
I must wander all alone,
Whilst the wild wave mocks my moan,
As it floats into this midnight of the year.

22

Down in sweet **Wyoming vale**
With a maiden sad and pale,
The joy to walk, no more to me is given;
For a bridegroom **from above**
Came and bore **away** my love,
And she walketh now a happy bride in Heaven.

WAR! WAR! WAR!

War! war! war!
  Thousands of people to lend;
War! war! war!
  Millions of treasure to spend;
Ne'er did the wealth of a nation thus flow,
To spread through its homes desolation and wo!

Blood! blood! blood!
  Oh! for the peace that has fled!
Blood! blood! blood!
  Oh! for the tears that are shed!
Shed by the silent hearths, lone and forsaken,
Where throb the lonely hearts, bleeding and breaking.

Wo! wo! wo!
  Hath God forsaken his people?
Wo! wo! wo!
  Hear the death-bell in the steeple!
In her lone chamber the maiden sits weeping;
Dead on the dark field her lover lies sleeping.

24

Peace! peace! peace!
  Spread thy bright pinions to-morrow;
Peace! peace! peace!
  O'er this wide nation of sorrow:
Come, and this torn land from conflict deliver,
Ere its last star sets in darkness forever.

I WILL COME TO THEE.

I will come to thee,—I will come to thee,
    In the visionary land;
As the breeze that fans the summer sea,
And stirs the boughs of the orange tree
    In the realms of golden sand,—
So softly whispered my love shall be.

I will come to thee, sweet one; I long
    To drink from thine azure eye;
To hear again the voice of song
Thou didst breathe for me, ere the world's deep wrong
    To our hopes came rushing by,
For thy tender heart, too strong,—too strong.

I will come to thee, when life hath fled;
    Not then in the land of dreams;
Not in the valley of the dead,—
But far beyond that bourne of dread,
    Where joy forever beams;
And tears are never,—never shed.

'THE CHAINED SEMINOLE.

'Tis past! and I am now a slave;
   The tall mast bends towards the west;
And gazing on the dark blue wave,
⁵I think upon my father's grave,
   And wish that I too were at rest.

⁶But yesterday, and I could claim
   The eagle feather for my brow:
Lord of a heart no fear could tame;
Men trembled when they heard my name;
   And now! these chains! what am I now?

My camp is by Kahawa's stream:
   My tribe still lingers on its shore;
To watch, beneath the pale moon's beam;
And hope,—vain hope, if they do deem
   He comes,—their chief will come no more.

And she,—my pride :—my " startled doe,"
   The wife I guarded well and long,
She sits where silent waters flow ;
And wails ;—and none can soothe her wo.
   Her heart is breaking on her song.

Well, let it break,—her native pine
   Will spread its branches o'er her grave,
And I, in dreams will seek that shrine;
And call her spirit back to mine,
   When sleeps my heart beyond the wave.

Nor ocean,—nor the white man's chain,
   Nor fate, can our true hearts divide.
The spirit hath a wide domain;
In death we soon shall meet again
   To roam the forests side by side.

THE MOON ON THE GREEN LEAF.

The moon on the green leaf shines bright, love :
The lone bird sings sad to the night, love :
And I have no sweeter delight, love,
Than to sing with the south winds to thee ;
  Would I could whisper as lowly ;
  And steal by thy lattice as slowly :
  And bathe with a spirit as holy,
That brow which is dearest to me.

Warm hearts were ne'er made for the day, love,
They pine when the stars fade away, love :
Then feast on to-night whilst you may, love.
Who knows what to-morrow may bring?
  Friends may depart who are nearest :
  Ties may be broken now dearest,
  And cold death may come which is drearest,
To shatter the hopes where we cling.

29

HOTULKA,

THE LAST OF THE UCHEES.

A WAIF OF THE FLORIDA EVERGLADES.

'Twas winter in that balmy clime,
  That wearies hearts with sunny hours;
Bright land, o'er which the hand of **time**
  But waves to scatter earth with flowers.
'Twas **winter**, but the birds sang on :
  And filled the forests with **their glee**;
What though the summer months were gone ?
  The vine still blossomed on the tree.

Bright are thy wilds, oh! Florida;
  And sweet thy breath at morning hour :
When 'wake the winds to **waft away**
  Rich perfume from each bud and **flower.**

'**Twas there one morn, when** Heaven gave
Her rosy torch to light the **wave**;
And **poured on wild-wood** waving green,
Her warming **flood** of golden sheen ;—

30

That on Paoka's shining breast,
  Full many a lovely island lay;
One,—far more lovely than the rest ;
  Out on the blue wave far away.
A light canoe upon its shore ;
A footprint, and a broken oar ;
Told that some lonely forest child,
  That morn had landed from the waves.
What sought he in that spot so wild ?
  That solitary isle of graves ?
No red man there his wigwam made ;
No red deer drank beneath its shade.
For fifty moons the glossy snake
Had lorded there, within the brake ;
And few the sounds that isle had heard,
Save wind, and wave, and frighted bird.
He came to gaze on that lone isle ;
  Once his forefathers' dwelling-place ;
To linger there, ere death, awhile ;
  Last of a darkly fated race !
His plume with battle smoke was black,
  He'd fled the field, but not in fear ;
Had heard the bloodhounds on his track ;
  Their baying still rang on his ear ;
Clenched on his breast his swarthy hands ;
His broken bow flung on the sands ;

His wampum on the cypress hung;
To which dark flesh and ringlet clung;
Torn from the brows of dying men,
'Midst shouts he ne'er would hear again.
The iron brow,—the lip of scorn :—
　　The heaving breast,—the eye of flame ;—
Told of a heart, howe'er forlorn,
　　That fate might crush, but could not tame.
Fell storms upon that brow had wrought
　　The lines deep sunk in its deadly lower :
And that wild eye its flame had caught,
　　O'er slaughtered heaps, in the battle hour.

He spoke,—but in a voice so low,
　　The passing breeze scarce caught the sound ;
'Twas to the dead he breathed his wo ;
　　Deeming their spirits hovering round :

"They come ! they come ! like ocean-waves,
　　For fifty moons these feet have pressed
The grassless earth of white men's graves :
　　And yet they come :—no rest,—no rest.
For fifty moons, amidst the pines
　　And by the lake, and by the stream,
I've seen them march their bannered lines
　　Bright shining 'neath the morning beam.

Through tears that never should have shamed
  The lightning of the red-man's eye,
I've gazed until my heart was tamed;
  As swept their heavy columns by.
It was not that I feared the might,
  When arm to arm the combat came,
Of those who'd heard above the fight,
  And trembled at Hotulka's name:
But oh! they brought the memory nigh,
Of days, when at my wild war-cry
With iron hearts, and ready hands,
  A legion would have thundered forth
To scourge them from our hunting lands,
  Back to their mountains in the North.
None answer now my battle call:
My tribe! my tribe! all cowards, all.
And think they that their chief will trace
The footsteps of his fallen race:—
Will cross the broad and briny wave,
  To seek beneath the white man's eye
A nameless and unhonored grave,
  With scarcely land on which to die?
No! father!—by thine ashes, no!
Nor longer will I fly the foe,
That now with many a glancing oar,
Is sweeping for this island shore:

The grass above thine honored head
Will bend beneath the white man's tread,
Ere thou and I together meet ;
     Alas! I have nor wife, nor child,
To watch the death-fire at my feet :
     Or weep me in the forest wild.
I stood and saw my infant boy
     Die on his famished mother's breast :
And then I laughed aloud with joy,
     To know that they would be at rest,
Whilst I could roam the wilds, to flood
And feed their memory with blood.

Last night, of leaf and moss I made
My bed deep in the hammock shade;
Whilst played the south-wind o'er my brow,
And stole the starlight through the bough :
The black wolf passed,—I heard his cry,
Go startling on the night-winds by:
And near the cypress shadowed stream,
I heard the prowling panther scream.
But sadly on my heart they fell,
Those sounds that once I loved so well;
Sadly and darkly,—till there came
A soft low voice, that breathed my name ;
It was no dream,—I saw that form

That always in the battle storm
Has hovered o'er me, when the cry
That swelled my heart, brought victory.

"Art thou my sister? speak! I cried,
    And tell me of the spirit-home;
And tell me of my own dark bride,
    And boy,—do they together roam?
And hath she taught his arm to bend
    The hunter's bow,—his eye so bright,
To aim the feathered shaft, and send
    It true upon the eagle's flight?
And tell me if, where ye are met,
    Beyond the sunless path of death,
The red man's spirit can forget
    The wrong that stilled his nation's breath.
Oh! speak! and bid my heart rejoice:
How softly fell that spirit voice!"

"Brother,—I have come for thee,
    From the land that knows no sorrow,—
Through death's wilderness with me,
    Thou must journey hence to-morrow;
Fearful is the way before thee,
    Serpents on thy path will lie;
Boughs of cypress will bend o'er thee;

'Lumined by the panther's eye;
Through the hammock dim and lone,
Where the glad sun never shone;
By the still and dark lagoon,
Never lit by star or moon,—
Thou must journey many days;
   Days of darkness unto thee;
For the welcome morning rays,
   On thy path thou shalt not see:
Yet no evil shall betide thee;
For a spirit-hand will guide thee,
Till death's cold and voiceless river
Parts thee and despair forever.

" Brother, come:—we wait for thee,
   Where the boughs wave dark and free;
   Where the stream is gently flowing;
   And the yellow corn is growing;
   Gems that glitter in the sun;
      Plumage from the eagle's wing;—
   Belts of wampum newly spun,
      Maids to deck thy form will bring;
   There, beneath the sunny skies,
   Unpursued the red deer flies;
   Here but evil spirits roam;
   Voices call thee,—brother, come."

"Hark! I hear the white man's oar;
  He is nearing now the shore;
  Father, they have trailed me far;
  By the sun, and by the star;
  Fast before them have I fled,
    Not Hotulka's blood to save,
    But to die upon thy grave;
  These sands a pillow for my head."

Twice twenty oars now broke the waves
That rolled along that isle of graves;
No other sound was on the deep;
  Firm stood the chief, with sombre brow;
On came the oars with steady sweep:
  Nearer:—They reach the shore:—and now
The hunters leap upon the sand:
Why pause they there, that armed band?
Too late:—despair hath struck the blow;
And men, who but an hour ago
Were wild for combat, now shrink back,
  As though a hand, they dared not name,
Had flung before their bloodhound track
  A sight to scorch their cheeks with shame.
There, bleeding on his father's grave,
  The Chieftain lay:—his dying eye
Fixed sternly on the far off wave,

As though he saw his Heaven nigh;
The human hunters 'round him close,
　Their footsteps wake him from his trance;
He turns his eyes upon his foes;
　" Would I could blast ye, with my glance!"
He wildly laughed; "I thought ye came
　For blood?—'tis here upon the sand:
Why pause ye there, with heart so tame,
　You! pale faced chieftain of the band?
Thine is the victor's trophy now:—
Come, tear it from my dying brow:
'Twill swell your fame where'er you roam:
And when you reach your mountain home,
There hang it on your gilded wall;
　'Twill make your coward children brave;
Boast to them, how ye slew us all;
　And made our land one mighty grave.
Behold my wampum on yon bough;
　'Tis decked with scalps of slaughtered dead.
The once bright ringlets, mark them now;
　See how the living gloss hath fled:
So may the lustre of your fame
　Grow dim when Indian wrongs are told;
And may your women cry out, "Shame!"
　And mock ye when your heart is old;
And may the Spirit of the sun,—

Him, ye call God,—the holy one,
Laugh out, and mock ye, when your cry
Is lifted up in agony,
From that dread hell, ye shrink to name;
Yet worship in your deeds of shame.

"The sun grows dim;—the wave looks dark:
   See, how the isles are reeling 'round!
The spirit voice arises,—hark!
   It calls me to the happy ground:
Sister!—I yield to thee my soul—
   I would not be a slave, to dwell,
Beneath a 'pale face' king's control,
   Robbed of these wilds I love so well.
See! see! they hover o'er my head!
   My wife! my child! no more to part—
I come!"
             Death sealed within his heart
The words, if more he would have said.

NEVER MORE.

Never more! never more!
Speak no word of farewell! shed no tear.

>> All is o'er.

Let us part in silence, kindly:
We have loved,—God knows how blindly:—

>> But 'tis past.

No words!—but I would ask
From those pale trembling lips

>> One kiss!—the last.

40

I THINK OF MY WIFE AND CHILD.

I think of my wife and child ;
   And I cannot sleep to-night ;
For the storm is up, and the winds are wild,
   And the ocean waves are white.
Oh ! watch them from the skies,
   God of the land and sea ;
And guide their bark, through the tempest dark,
   For we put our trust in Thee.

When we rest on the quiet land,
   We forget, 'midst the pleasures there,
That Thou hold'st in thy mighty hand,
   Our rapture, and our despair.
But out on the howling deep,
   'Midst the wail of the frantic wave,
We own thy might, to the wild midnight,
   And trust to Thine arm to save.

Oh ! Thou who on Galilee
   Didst say to the wave, " Be still ! "
When the strong arm failed, and the stout heart quailed,
   And the wave obeyed Thy will,—

41

Oh! watch from thy Father's throne,
  And guard on this fearful sea,
My wife and child, through the midnight wild,
  Is the prayer I lift to Thee.

GREEN LEAVES ARE ABOVE ME.

Green leaves are above me, to gladden my eye,
Though the summer is past, and November gone by;
Glad song-birds the green boughs with melody fill,
And sunlight is dancing on prairie and hill:
But the morn hath awakened a thrill in my heart,
No song-bird or sunlight could ever impart;
     For a mantle of white
      Hath been spread through the night
O'er all the wide valleys, o'er all the high hills.

The voices of playmates, forgotten for years,
Now fall with the ringing of bells, on my ears;
My ruddy cheeked brother;—I see him once more:
And his track in the snow, 'round our own cottage
    door;
Though white is his shroud, as the snow on the plain,
He lives in my heart, and is with me again.
And there is my sister,—with cheek like the dawn,
     And soft beaming eyes,
     Like the blue of the skies:
But sad is the whisper, that she too is gone.

When again shall I 'wake to such mornings of joy,
As lit up the snow plains, when I was a boy?
When again will I shout, from the old snow-clad mill
To wake up the echo that slept on the hill?

When my childhood returns;—when the hand of
    decay,
Flings back the dark locks long ago snatched away;
When the griefs that are seared on my heart and my
    brain
                Are no more:—from the tomb,
                In the dream that may come,
I may shout to the hill and the echo again.

COME, SOLDIERS, FILL UP!

Come, soldiers, fill up! and let wine make **amends**
   For the **toils** we have suffered to-day;
And deep from our hearts, let **us** pledge to old friends,
   Whom we cherish, though **far**, far away.

There's a **chord** in the soldier's heart, ever the same,
   That awakes at the bivouac fire,
When touched by the sound of an old comrade's name,
   A music more sweet than the lyre.

Oh! what were this life, if 'twere not for the past?
   The present—a flash, and 'tis gone;
The future—a sea, on which only **are cast**
   False beacons, to beckon **us on.**

Time scatters more sorrow than joy from his wing,
   But with wine, **we** may laugh at his flight:
So fill up! whatever the future may bring,
   Let joy gild the goblet to-night.

SANIHO OLD.

"Saniho" old is a warrior bold,
   And his hair has grown gray from years :
You'd swear on the book, at the very first look,
   That it never grew gray from fears.

A besom of wrath, on the wild war path,
   He swept in his manhood's prime :
But his pace is now slow ; for he's crankie below ;
   And his *physique* has served out its time.

He is cousin by blood to Prince "Buffalo Cud"
   And grandsire to "Buffalo Hump."
His wife's a Tonkway,—with the soft sobriquet
   Of "The lizard that sleeps on the stump."

He enjoys the free air, when the weather is fair ;
   And creeps into his Lodge when it rains :
He is fond of dog-stew,—but he dotes on ragout,
   Of mule meat, mixed with warriors' brains.

In lieu of red beads, as a sign of brave deeds,
   He wears, when in courtly attire,
Three grim looking rows of white teeth from the foes
   Who have fallen beneath his grim ire.

He'd a virtue most rare, in the dark of his hair,
   That is,—ere his locks had grown white ;
For from rag-tail to chief, so accomplished a thief
   Never emptied a halter at night.

Alas! his high fame, and his heroic name,
   Are eclipsed in these heroic times ;
There are robbers more bold, if the truth were but
     told,
   But their names shall be nameless in rhymes.

ON THE WAVE OF THE NUÉCES.

On the wave of the Nuéces
   Shines the cold October moon ;
And the spirit of the west wind
   Sweeps o'er moorland and lagoon :
Sad is the ocean's wailing ;
   Mournful and sad to me :
As I think upon my lone wife,
   Far in the north countree.

A tear drop in her dark eye,—
   Does it gather there for me,
O'er her baby on her bosom,
   Looking up so smilingly ?
Oh ! wrap that jewel closely,
   For 'twas born midst tropic flowers ;
And keep the fagots blazing
   Through the snowy midnight hours.

My heart is sadly beating ;
   Yet my blood flows warm the while :
And though I feel like weeping,
   I but think of home, and smile.

Let others love the zephyrs,
  But give, oh! give to me
The winds that howl through winter,
  Far in the north countree.

I HEAR THE WINDS WHISTLE.

I hear the winds whistle, I hear the loud wave ;
And I sit by my hearthstone, and think of the grave :
The eyes that are sunken,—the brows that are cold :
The lips that are faded,—the shroud and the mould.

The fagot burns brightly, but deep in my heart,
Dwells a spirit of darkness that will not depart ;
And it calls up old faces,—and looks that they wore
Ere the grim robber, Death, cast his shade at my door.

When his dark shadow falls on my threshold again,
I shall smile in his face, as I yield to his chain ;
For my old eyes grow dim, and I no longer care
To be watching the fagot that's flickering there.

I hear the winds whistle,—I hear the loud wave,
And I sit by the hearthstone, and think of the grave :
The eyes that are sunken,—the brows that are cold,
The lips that are faded,—the shroud and the mould.

STREAM OF THE MOUNTAIN.

Stream of the mountain region! still the same;
   Thy voice goes upward, as thy wave rolls on.
When first my lip was taught to breathe thy name,
   I loved thee,—and I blessed thee :—when the dawn
Of youth first bade my childhood dreams depart,
Thy voice first spoke of God to my young heart.

I'm here, in manhood now :—and as I gaze,
   Along thy placid breast, my tears fall fast;
My spirit wanders back to those bright days,
   When thou and I were playmates :—when I cast
My mimic bark, to brave thy fitful vein,
And thou wouldst smile, and toss it back again.

The laugh of youth then rang along thy shore ;
   Eyes lit by hope, beamed joyful on thy wave.
By rock and tree that laugh is heard no more :
   Young hearts and hopes lie buried in the grave.
Lost ones ;—you were the world to me,—and now,
I read your names beneath the willow bough.

51

Down to thy sunny beach how oft they came,
　　To gather pebbles in their childish glee :
They're silent now !—but thou art still the same,
　　Thy voice as solemn, and thy wave as free :
Thy music steals to where their graves are spread.
What wave will sing for me, when I am dead ?

I go to where the orange shades the tomb,
　　In that bright land where summer never dies ;
Amidst its flowers death loses half its gloom :
　　There blossoms fall, with every breath that sighs,—
But when the parting bell shall toll for me :
Bright stream !—my soul will wander back to thee.

BOAT SONG.

Let us rest on our oars,—the sky is bright,
The winds are hushed, and our hearts are light:
Let us rest on our oars, and be happy while
We float by the shore of our own green isle;
And merrily sing our evening song,
To the silent woods as we glide along.

'Tis daylight yet,—See, the sun still shines
On the verdant tops of the island pines;
Then why should we toil? we have naught to fear,
For the stream is swift, and our homes are near,
Where the smiles are bright, and the hearth is red;
And our evening meal on the board is spread.

The monarch sits on his gilded throne,
And deems the world and its joys his own:
But happier, though *he* wears a crown,
Are *we*, on our oars, when the sun goes down,
And our song of love to the evening star,
On the silent shore is heard afar.

But see :—through the hemlock, a dancing light.
There is joy in the Creole's hut to-night;
Hark! hark! how the shout of glee rings out;
There are younger hearts than our wives' about:
Now ply the oar, and arouse the foam,
And a merry cheer for the boatman's home.

OH! WAKE FROM THY DREAMING.

Oh! wake from thy dreaming;
The starlight is beaming;
And drinking the dew from the bud and the bough.
Oh! wake from thy sleeping,
For fond eyes are keeping
Their watch with the heavens that smile o'er thee now.
The heart that is lonely,
That sighs for thee only;
But kindles to joy when it feels thou art near:
Then treat not with spurning
The lip that is burning
To tell all it feels, to thy listening ear.

Oh! come with thy lover,
The green boughs will cover
Our way through the glen where the winds are at rest.
My steed on the prairie,
Is waiting to bear thee,
O'er flower and fern, to a home in the West;
Where we'll lose all life's sadness
In bright dreams of gladness;

Forget all the past in the joys of to-day:

  And never,—oh! never,

  'Till death bids us sever,

Lend a breath of our love to the wing of decay.

ON THE WILD WIDE MISSISSIPPI.

On the wild wide Mississippi
  The moon is shining down,
And her lustre gilds the ripple,
  As we float by yonder town.
I am dreaming—but 'tis folly;
  I am hoping, but 'tis vain,
Whilst a thousand miles between us lie
  Of forest, wave, and plain.

Like the moon upon the water,
  Memory lights my spirit here;
Like the voice of night, her whisper
  Falls in sweetness on my ear:
But the stream is dark before me,
  And I cannot cast my eyes
On the shadow of the future
  That before me darkly lies.

As o'er the stream and valley
  Floats the rosy breath of June,
Peace woos me to her bosom,
  But my heart is out of tune,

57

For I feel beneath this starlight,
  Whilst my eyes are weeping rain,
That beneath the stars of Heaven
  We shall never meet again.

THE MULE'S LAMENT.

Know ye the land where the river St. Johns
  Rolls on through the palm forest to the salt sea;
Where Sol gilds the mule yard when morning first
    dawns,
  And the sheds that give shade to my brothers and
    me?

Through its hammocks and forests, for many a day,
  Have I toiled o'er the sands for my pitiful grain;
And sighed at my trough till my tail has grown gray,
  And sweat for my country, again and again.

When the war-whoop was heard in the pine shadowed
    wood;
  When the drivers all ran, and the fight was a race,
Like a Holy Cross knight, in my harness I stood,
  Calmly smiling at fate—with my leg o'er the trace.

'Midst this donkey brevetment, oh! where my reward?
  Ungroomed and unshodden,—faint, foundered, and
    sick:

The first transport that passes will bear me on board,
  Floating down the St. Johns, to be sold at Black
    Creek.

My brothers in toil, yet uncrushed by the chains,
  Be warned by my fate;—this your doom I foretell:
When the war trumpets cease, for your service and
    pains,
  You'll be sold at Black Creek, by the auctioneer
    Bell.

THE NORTH WIND.

It moans o'er the prairie,
  It sighs through the brake;
It roars in the forest,
  It howls on the lake;
'Tis laden with sorrow,
  Pale Poverty's sigh;
And the groan of the houseless
  It bears through the sky.

It scatters the brown leaves
  That autumn hath shed;
It sighs o'er the branches
  That wave o'er the dead;
It shakes the low cabin
  Where burns the pale light,
To cheer her who watcheth
  The tempest to-night.

The pride of her bosom
  Is out on the deep;
And the noise of the billow
  Forbids her to sleep;

For the blast to her slumber
  Its wrath would impart;
And the cry of the shipwrecked
  Would ring on her heart.

'Tis now at the altar,
  And now stealing in,
Where the felon lies fettered
  In iron and sin;
Now high on the mountain;
  Now down in the vale;
And the mad ocean heareth
  Its desolate wail.

Howl on! To the sinful
  Thy voice hath a charm;
And thy spirit inciteth
  The murderer's arm;
No whisper of conscience—
  No terror of God—
As he moveth in silence
  And darkness abroad.

We own Thee, our Father;
  We know 'tis thy hand
That guideth the tempest
  O'er ocean and land;

And yet do we tremble
  And shrink at thy might;
Though we know, whatsoever
  Thou doest is right.

THINK NOT OF ME.

Think not of me when morning breaks
  In glory o'er earth's laughing streams;
Think not of me when morning wakes
  Thy spirit from the land of dreams;
Nor when afar, the evening star
  Shines through the dying light of day;
Nor when you gaze upon its rays
  That through the twilight forest plays.

Think not of me when mirth is high,
  And wine upon the lip is bright;
Think not of me when those are nigh
  Who watch thy smile with love's delight;
When joy beams rest within thy breast,
  And sunlit hours like moments flee;
When earth can throw no shade of wo
  Across thy soul—no thought of me!

But think of me in gloomy night,
  When sorrow sits upon thy pillow;
When grief that clouds thy spirits light,
  Rolls o'er thy bosom like a billow;

When hopes far fled,—friends false or dead,
   Have left a cheerless world to thee;
Relief most dear,—the burning tear!
   Then, midst the gloom,—one thought of me.

THE BEAUTIFUL SKY.

The beautiful sky! Since I wandered a boy
By the blue Susquehanna, I've watched it with joy;
The living in sorrow, the dead in their shrouds,
Have never yet robbed me of joy in the clouds.

Aurora may dress up the mountains in gold,
And on the wide waters her crimson unfold;
Or shake from her mantle the dew like a shower,
To deck out in jewels earth's every flower;

Yet God is not there, in his glory and might,
But far up in the clouds, where he pours out his light;
Where the sun, as he sinks in his glory to rest,
Pours flame 'round the armies that march in the West.

God gave me in mercy, two homes with my breath:
In one I must toil to the portals of death;
Ah! when shall I lay down my sorrows and fly
To the home of my soul, in the beautiful sky.

OH! LADY, BREATHE THAT SONG AGAIN.

Oh! lady, breathe that song again!
  To those who idly list to thee;
It may be but an idle strain,
  But oh! a mournful joy to me;
Less welcome to the violet blue,
Is the first drink of morning dew,
The breeze that spreads its leaves apart,
Than that low music to my heart.

I feel as when I heard it first;
  And oh! methinks a sister's eye
Beams in my own, as it did erst,
  When childhood's days went dancing by.
I see the lofty mountain pine,
That whispered o'er her home and mine:
Alas! the willow branches wave
In sadness now above her grave.

Oh! lady, wake those notes again,
  Nor heed my tears, though they should flow,
Whilst steal across my dreaming brain
  Sad memories of long ago;

And when afar, in after time,
I think of thee in distant clime,
I'll pledge to one whose minstrelsy
Could bring my childhood back to me.

THE MARINER'S WIFE.

How wildly now the north-wind blows;
 The drifting snow the pale moon hides;
How dark the frown of ocean grows;
 I wonder where my husband bides:
Now toils he on the mountain wave,
 Or clings he to some rocky shore;
Or have the mermaids spread his grave,
 Far down beneath the billow's roar?

These blasts such terrors o'er me bring,
 I dare not close my eyes in sleep;
For if I do, my thoughts will wing
 Their way unto the crazy deep;
And frightful rocks, and wrecks, and men
 In dying strife, I'll there behold,
And every yawning wave will then
 New terrors to my view unfold.

Sleep on, my babe;—thou dost not know
 The risk thy father dares for thee;
Thy little cheek would lose its glow
 Could those soft eyes his danger see;

Yet thou wilt be a sailor too,
   And heedless of the ocean wave,
Soon wilt thou love the billows blue,
   And learn to laugh where tempests rave.

But hark! the winds are falling now;
   Hope comes upon their dying song;
Sleep's shadow steals across my brow,
   Where fears have hovered all night long.
Where'er my husband's bark doth ride,
   On stormy bay, or ocean's breast,
Kind Fortune, ever there abide;
   And Hope, be thou his constant guest.

WHEN THE MOON.

When the moon looks down through silent night,
  On wood, and tower, and stream,
I think of thee,—my bosom's light,
  Star of my life's dark dream;
And if, in the triumph of hope over fear,
There falls from the font of remembrance a tear,
                    Mary, receive it;
And if it tells of a heart as true
To thee as the stars to the Heavens blue,
                    Mary, believe it.

THE DUELIST AT SEA.

Ye midnight winds, whose howlings wake
   Within my breast this stormy joy:
Breathe madness in these waves that make
   A plaything of this ocean toy;
And lift her, till the hosts of stars
   Seem reeling from their homes in Heaven;
Till groan the masts, and bend the spars,
   And flap the sails, in tatters riven.

There drives across my brain a woe
   More terrible than ocean's wrath;
When life is journeying too slow
   For all the tempests on its path,
Then cleave the angry waves apart;
   Dash high the phosphorescent light;
The blood leaps madly to this heart,
   That would not brook a calm to-night.

I feel a joy in all things wild;
   God spare me from the silent land,
Or make me once again a child,
   And wash this blood stain from my hand;

Upward I dare not turn my eyes;
   A shrouded form forever sails
Between my dark soul and the skies,
   O'er which a frantic mother wails.

A brother's curse—a sister's scream—
   Break on my ear when quiet reigns;
And like a burning lava stream,
   The hot blood rushes through my veins;
But here, upon the howling deep,
   As through the midnight storm we scud,
I'll brave it, though the angels weep,
   And all their raining tears are blood.

SING NOT OF HOME!

Sing not to me of home! I've stood
  Once more within my native dell,
Where falls the light on waving wood,
   And cliff and stream remembered well.
Beneath the verdant ivy bower
I've watched the bee upon the flower,
And heard from out the locust tree,
The skylark's morning melody
Fall sweetly on my ear, as when,
To joy I ne'er can know again,
It woke me from my boyhood sleep,
   To ramble forth through grove and bower,
And gather, by the mountain steep,
   The berry red, and dewy flower.

Sing not of home! But yesterday
I could have listened to thy lay;
For I had cherished in my brain
   A wild delusion—false as sweet;
I thought, when I beheld again
My native mountain, stream, and plain,
   Despair and I would no more meet.

An exile, with an ocean wide
 Between me and my native land;
For long, long years my spirit sighed
 For that sweet hour when I should stand
Again where sleeps the mountain breeze
Among my own bright forest trees.

Alas! alas! I little thought   .
That hour would be with anguish fraught;
That in one glance the hope would perish,
My soul so long had loved to cherish.
 My sister's cheek was bright and fair;
  My brother's heart was warm and brave;
 The myrtle crowns the hillock where
  They sleep together in one grave;
 And many a morning dew hath wet
  The grass above my father's head;
 And where no blade hath sprung up yet,
  My mother sleeps:—God rest the dead!
 And she—the flower and pride of all
  Who mingled in the moonlight dance—
 My young love:—in a stranger's hall
  I met her cold and careless glance.
 But thanks to Heaven for that one joy,
  She knew me not,—no eye could trace
 The features of the laughing boy
  Upon my dark and altered face.

Thus to my childhood home I came;
   A stranger :—knowing, but unknown :
Heard many a well remembered name;
   Breathed only to the dead my own.
No kindred now with man I claim,
   But in the wide world stand alone.

My boat waits on the beach **below**;
   My spirit sighs for wave and foam:
One song from thee before **I go**;
   But not of home—oh! not of home.

WHEN FAR, FAR AWAY.

When far, far away, from thy prairie bride,
    And her home by the setting sun,
Wilt thou think how she gathered, with eager hands,
The choicest flowers of the prairie lands,
To sweeten the air where her wigwam stands,
    Ere our evening joys begun?

Thou didst tell her once—and she, joyful, wept,
    For a truth thy dark eye wore—
Thou wouldst not exchange the prairie wild,
The sun-bright home of Manoneen's child,
For the brightest joy that ever smiled
    On thy wayward path before.

But now, when the green leaves fade and fall,
    And the north-winds drift the sand,
Like the bird that comes with the spring-time flower,
To gladden our hearts in the sun-lit hour,
Thou dost fly from the autumn tinted bower
    To a warmer and brighter land.

Thy love—no more in the still blue lake
    Will she gaze, with laughing eyes;
Nor paint her cheek, nor braid her hair;
Nor flatter her heart that she is fair;
Nor dream that thine hath its dwelling where
    The rose on her brown cheek lies.

But go,—and when those arms of thine
    Infold a fairer bride,
Forget not her who, void of art,
Gave freely to thee all her heart;
But when she saw thy form depart,
     Shamed not her father's pride.

ON LEAVING THE ST. LAWRENCE.

Up springs the breeze! The isles are passed;
Good night! good night! we part at last:
Thou restless stream, whose ceaseless song,
    Since daylight fell upon thy shore,
Hath taught me, as we swept along,
    Each hour to love thee more and more.
When my first glance I threw on thee,
    My heart grew light, for o'er my brain
There stole a silent memory
    That brought my childhood back again,
With all its joyful hopes and flowers;
    And voices, nigh forgotten, came,
To cheer my sad and lonely hours,
    And whisper of a brighter name
Than e'er was won on earth, to shine
Upon ambition's hollow shrine.

Peace to thy sunny banks of green,
And each blue wave that rolls between!
I've cast upon thee tears and smiles,
Bright River of a Thousand Isles;

I've watched thee with a lover's eye;
I leave thee with a lover's sigh:
For thou has o'er my spirit cast
A joy not felt since childhood passed.

His song of home the steersman sung,
As swept our bark the isles among;
And midst the forest green we heard
The rushing wing of joyful bird;
The bee was busy on the flower,
The thrush was merry in her bower;
Earth seemed to wear a gladness new;
And my lone heart was joyful too.

'Tis strange, how old familiar sounds
   Bring back the light of buried years;
And how departed joy rebounds,
   To fill stern eyes with childish tears;
The peasant's halloo from the hill;
The murmur of some laughing rill;
The merry carol of a bird;
Or aught that childhood's ear hath heard.

Good night! good night! Thou chainless stream,
Whilst stars look on thee with their gleam,
My spirit grieves to think we part;
For thou hast twined around my heart,

And stolen half the love it bore
For that bright one, whose silent shore
First woke me to a dream of Him
Who sits among the cherubim,
And oft gave back, in cadence long,
The echo of my boyhood song.

      Good night!

THE BEREAVED.

The sun shines through my window,
  The sky is bright and clear;
God's smile is all around me,
  His voice rings on my ear;
But mine eyes are wet with weeping,
  And my heart is sad and drear.

I would the sky were darker;
  I would the song-bird's strain,
That floats into my chamber
  From the orchard and the plain,
Would cease, and never mock me
  With its melody again.

Though joy hath fled forever,
  Though I in summer cast
On one pale, earthly flower,
  Too frail for autumn's blast,
My heart and its affections,
  I would not recall the past.

The chair she used, sits vacant;
  The wreath that decked her brow,
When at **the** bridal altar
  Her young lip breathed the **vow,**
And each trembling word was music,
  Fades 'neath **my** tear drops now.

Alas! they're ever falling,
  Since she, my life, hath **flown;**
Yet oh! I'd rather weep her,
  Than never to have known
The **love** that filled her bosom
  And in her dark eyes shone.

SWEET WAS THE DREAM.

Sweet was the dream of my own bright land,
  Where the roses never die;
I saw the green banks where the palm trees stand,
  And the glad stream murmuring by;
The jasmine green on the garden wall;
  The hills in the sunshine clad,
And the verdant leaves that never fall,
  To make the heart grow sad.

The voice of the dancing rill I heard,
  And the sigh of the evening breeze;
And the song of the merry mocking-bird
  In the golden orange trees.
My aged mother kissed my cheek,
  And my sister weeping came,
With trembling lips, that scarce could speak
  Her long lost brother's name.

Softly she breathed, 'tween voice and sigh,
  "Thou wilt part from us no more;
The tears of grief on our cheeks we'll dry,
  Since sorrow for thee is o'er.

Thou'lt stay for the hearts that love thee here—"
    The promise my lips had given;
When the sentry's voice smote on my ear,
    And my dream went back to Heaven.

I rose from my pillow:—The waning moon
    Shone dim through the broken cloud;
From the cold white hills the tempest tune
    Swept, mournfully and loud.
To a day of toil broke the morning beam;
    But lightly its labors fled,
For the sky I saw in my midnight dream,
    Its dew on my hopes had shed.

LEONORE.

I know that I am weaving now,
A wreath of anguish for my brow,
And kindling in my breast a blaze,
To scorch my heart in after days.
I see love's ashes in the urn;
And yet I cannot, cannot turn
From eyes that dazzle whilst they burn—
      The eyes of sweet Leonore.

I'm floating in a summer dream
Of joy, adown love's burning stream,
To where the tempest clouds roll o'er
The hurtling wave and wreck-strewn shore;
The hour is near when we must part;
Its shadows gather o'er my heart:
Gleams through the gloom the fatal dart,
      That's winged by false Leonore.

Farewell to peace:—farewell to love;
The darkness gathers 'round, above;
Forever I have lost the light
Of eyes that made this world so bright;

There shines no star by which to guide
My bark adown the troubled tide.
Heartbroken now I wander wide
     From peace and false Leonore.

THEY DID NOT LAST.

They did not last! they did not last,
   Those joys that filled my youthful heart:
They all are buried with the past;
   I thought not then they would depart,
When first I learned to love the air
That fanned my brow and stirred my hair;
Rambling among the mountains wild,
A careless, lightsome, laughing child:
When first my spirit went abroad,
   To marvel at the mystery
Of nature, and of nature's God,
   Whom mortal eyes can never see:
I've watched the storm with crazy joy,
And laughed,—because I was a boy,
And thought it only hurtled there,
To mock the sun with crazy glare.
I saw not from the rocky steep
The mariner upon the deep;
A plaything for the frantic wave,
That soon would roll above his grave.

And then I wished the very strings
  That held my life were torn asunder;
That God would give my spirit wings,
  To soar beyond the realm of thunder.

I've watched the stars, until I've felt
  The hot tears to my young eyes stealing;
And nursed such thoughts as seemed to melt
  My soul with wild delicious feeling.

O, Earth and Heaven!—But 'tis strange,
How time can work this wond'rous change;
Now I look upon the sky
With a cold and careless eye:
When the stars are beaming brightly;
When the winds are whispering lightly;
Not the shining star or cloud
  Can a single joy impart;
Nothing makes my spirit proud;
  Worldly things have chained my heart;
Joys that with my boyhood past;
Why—oh! why, did ye not last?

WITHERED LILIES.

Withered lilies! withered lilies!
　　Once how bright ye were;
When the waters smiled around ye,
　　When ye floated there;
When each breeze that whispered o'er ye,
　　Kissed your leaves so green,
And your snowy buds and blossoms
　　Rocked the waves between.

Withered lilies! withered lilies!
　　Where's your glory gone?
Rock ye when the winds sweep o'er ye?
　　Smile ye when they're flown?
No:—your element forsook ye;
　　False the waters were;
This, the ebbing wave hath told ye:
　　"Weep and wither there."

Emblems of the broken-hearted,
　　Such to me ye seem;
Tears your yellow leaves have started,
　　Bitter as life's dream:

Yon bright sun, that once refreshed,
  Now sears ye with his ray;
Winds that nursed ye, now sweep o'er ye,
  Hastening your decay.

Thus when man, by hope forsaken,
  Sees all joy depart;
Things that once sweet thoughts could waken,
  Wither up his heart;
And he lingers like ye, wasting,
  On a cheerless shore;
Ne'er again of Heaven tasting,
  Warmed to life no more.

THE REAPERS ARE BINDING THEIR
SHEAVES IN THE GLEN.

The reapers are binding their sheaves in the glen;
The glad birds keep tune with the songs of the men;
There is joy:—but no joy to this heart comes again,
    Since Willie, my jewel, hath flown:
Gone, gone from the valley the light it once wore;
And the sunshine that into my heart used to pour;
For his voice will be heard 'mong the reapers no more;
    And I am alone :—all alone.

My mother looks strange when I sigh at my wheel,
For she knows not nor dreams of the anguish I feel;
Nor the tear that at night down my pillow doth steal,
    Since Willie, my jewel, hath flown.
Oh! bright was his eye, as the summer sun's beam,
And sweet was his voice as the whispering stream;
Oh! why did he rock me in love's tender dream,
    Then leave me to weep all alone.

But hark! in the grove there's a footstep draws near;
There's no step but Willie's e'er fell on my ear
Could make music like that; oh! I tremble with fear;
    I am weak since my Willie hath flown.

Yes! yes! 'tis his voice, and he calls on my name;
My words were unkind; and he still is the same:
Oh! Willie forgive—I was all, all to blame;
   You will leave me no more, all alone.

OH! IS THIS THE VALLEY?

Oh! is this the valley, and do I again
See the home of my childhood, I sighed for in vain,
When I stood by the hearthstone of strangers, and
    wept,
Whilst sorrow her haunt in my young bosom kept?

Yes, this is the valley:—But where is the joy
That made it all sunshine when I was a boy?
The whoop from the wild-wood, the laugh on the lawn;
And my rosy cheeked play-fellows, where are they
    gone?

I see the white cottage in which I was born,
And the hills where the white mists hung heavy at
    morn;
And I hear the glad song of the fountain below,
The same song I listened to summers ago.

'Tis sad to me now, as 'twas sweet to me then:
There came laughing ones here who will come not
    again;
I call on the name of my sister—Alas!
How sadly it dies on the winds as they pass.

Where now is that sister? yon churchyard can tell;
Yon bell tolled her parting; I heard not the knell;
Nor the knell for my brother, who sleeps by her side.
Alas! I was far, far away when they died.

I came here a stranger; I thought but to gaze
Once more on the home of my innocent days;
To wander unmoved through the silent green wood,
That o'ershawdows the stream, where the lost ones
     have stood.

I came here a stranger; I thought 'twould be joy,
In my manhood to roam where I roamed when a boy.
I have learned what deep sorrow a day may impart,
With the shadow of graves hanging over the heart.

THE BRIDGE HAS BEEN SWEPT
AWAY.

Along the shore!—along the shore,
  I wander by night and by day;
But alas! alas! I shall never cross o'er,
  For the bridge has been swept away;
And the stream is cold, and deep, and dark,
  And the bridge has been swept away.

Once I walked along the stream,
  Beauty and youth by my side;
Walked with one, my world's bright dream,
  Who was to have been my bride;
Alas! death came with his icy boat,
  And drifted her down the tide.

Beyond, the gardens were bright and green;
  Here all is brown and sear;
Beyond, the angel of hope was seen;
  Alas! he never comes here;
Beyond, I sometimes wept with joy;
  Now, I never shed a tear.

Along the shore!—along **the** shore,

   I wander by night and by day:

But alas! alas! I shall **never cross** o'er,

   For the bridge has **been swept** away;

And the stream is deep, and **dark,** and wild,

   And the bridge has been **swept away.**

THE NIGHT OF PALO-ALTO.

Let us rest on the sod,
 Whilst the moon shines bright;
We have nothing to fear
 From our foes to-night.
On the battle-stained field,
 Where their dead are strewn,
They have plenty of work,
 'Neath the midnight moon.
Hark! 'tis the sound
 Of the mattock and spade,
Breaking the ground
 By the chaparral shade.
God! whilst thy zephyrs
 Are over us sighing,
Grant peace to the dead,
 Send hope to the dying.

The neigh of the steed,
 As he plunges in gore,
O'er the rider who sleeps,
 To awake never more;

And the howl of the wolf,
　As he sits by the dead,
Full gorged on the banquet
　Man's passion hath spread,
Fill sadly the ear;
　But the heart dares not feel,
Whilst victory still hangs
　On its valor and steel.
When the morning light breaks
　Over yesterday's slain,
Each arm must be strong
　For the conflict again.
Then pour thy soft dreams
　On our hearts' gentle sleep,
But spare us from those
　Who await but to weep;
Whose heartstrings will break
　When the news shall be told
Of the graves that this night
　Have been dug on the wold.

Oh! mournful it is
　When a battle is done,
When a field hath been lost
　And a field hath been won:
To gaze on the face—

That can beam nevermore;
And call up the smile
 That it yesterday wore;
To press the cold hand
 That in life we oft pressed,
And know that its pulse
 Is forever at rest.
But sadder the trial
 For him who must bear
To the widow and orphan
 The words of despair.

'Tis sweet when the glad note
 Of fame fills the ears;
But sad when it floats
 O'er an ocean of tears.

MY THOUGHTS ARE NOW ON THEE.

My thoughts are now on thee, Mary;
   And my heart is far away,
Where the night-winds stir the linden boughs,
   That 'round thy lattice play;
And musing lonely here, Mary,
   So strange the currents run
Of thought, that smile and tear, Mary,
   Are melted into one.

No starlight falls on brighter lands,
   On brighter lands than thine;—
Whilst here upon the desert sands,
   No sadder home than mine.
Yet wildly dance my thoughts, and free,
   And lightly throbs my heart,
When dreaming that thou think'st of me,
   Though we are far apart.

A thousand hearts are dreaming now
   On yonder tented plain,
Of ones beloved—in far-off homes—
   They ne'er may see again;

But hope, in every soldier's breast,
   Shines like yon burning star,
That watches, whilst in midnight rest,
   He dreams of home afar.

'I'M STANDING BY THY DWELLING, BLAKE.

I'm standing by thy dwelling, Blake,
   Thy mansion dark and cold;
I come for old affection's sake,
   One hour with thee to hold.
The living, when my tears are free,
   Have claims above the dead;
Therefore I will not weep o'er thee
   Or hopes that with thee fled;
But whilst the waves of sorrow break
   All darkly on my heart,
I'll stand above thy dwelling, Blake,
   And dream o'er what thou wert.
The loved,—the generous,—the brave;
   None knew thy heart so well,
As he who now looks on thy grave
   Beside the chaparral.

There moves a mighty martial host
   By yonder rushing stream;
A mighty host,—whose banners boast
   Of conquest whilst they gleam;

But many hearts will sleep in dust,
   Before our foemen yield;
And those bright arms will lie in rust,
   On many a battle field.
The darkest fortune may be mine;
   It rests alone with God,
Who fills a lonely grave like thine,
   Beneath the prairie sod.

But whilst my blood flows warmly, Blake,
   And lives within my heart
One throb, for old affection's sake,
   I'll think o'er what thou wert,
And mourn that one so generous,
   So noble and so brave,
Should find a rest so early
   In a lonely prairie grave.

LA MUERTA DE RESACA.

When the Mexicans were flying
    From the Palo Alto plain;
From the groaning of their dying,
    From the silence of their slain;
Low, on the cold earth bleeding,
    Where by ruthless hands she fell,
Lay a maiden fair and lovely,
    'Midst the tangled chaparral.

Fair her dark brow of beauty;
    Her robeless breast more fair;
And shining as the raven's wing
    Her dark and braided hair;
And features that the sculptor's hand
    Might strive to trace in vain,—
In death's pale marble slumbered there,
    Beside that field of slain.

None knew if that pale lip had been
    The seat of truth or guile;
For none could read the mystery
    That slept beneath its smile;

None marvelled at her death,
  None asked the story of her life,
Or by what ruthless hand she fell,
  Or whether maid or wife.

She caught a passing glance from all,
  But no one paused to sigh;
For Resaca de la Palma,
  Rushed the maddened columns by;
And the only smile that upward went,
  Amidst that battle storm,
Was where the smoke went rolling
  O'er that lovely maiden's form.

That night the wreath of glory sat
  On many a hero's brow;
And deeds of those heroic men
  We hear them tell of now;
Their sounding fame through all the land
  Rings out with trumpet tone;
But the fame of that heroic girl
  Lives with her God alone.

THE BURIAL OF RINGGOLD.

Whilst the evening winds are blowing;
Whilst our tears are sadly flowing;
With his sword upon his breast,
Bear the soldier to his rest.
Whilst the summer leaves are singing
  Requiems for the fallen brave;
Where the prairie flowers are springing,
  Lay him in his honored grave.

When his death is told to-morrow,
  Where the shouts of battle swell,
Many a tear will fall in sorrow
  O'er the guns he loved so well.
But their steeds will dash more proudly
  O'er the field of smoke and fire;
And those guns will ring more loudly,
  Calling for a vengeance dire.

Tidings of this day of glory
  Soon o'er freedom's land will spread;
But a cloud will dim the story,
  When they tell of Ringgold dead:

None e'er knew him but to love him;
  For his heart was warm and brave;
Gently lay the sod above him;
  Glory's price :—a prairie grave.

PALO ALTO, *May 9th,* **1847.**

"WHAT IS A BREVET?"

As Captain Forbes walked off parade,
Sam Green inquiringly said:
"Pray tell me, Cap.,—and tell me true,
Why all those officers in blue
Walk up and touch their caps to you;
They've leaves and eagles, them 'ere chaps,
Whilst you've but bars upon your straps."
"Why, Sam," says Forbes, "you *must* be green;
The reason's plainly to be seen:—
My straps, so humble in their place,
Are worth the symbol on their face,
Whilst leaves and eagles pay no debts:—
Those officers are all brevets."
Says Green, "that puzzles me,—you bet;—
Cap, tell me,—what is a brevet?"
"Well, Sam,—to put it through your pate,
You listen, whilst I illustrate.
You see yon turkey on the fence:—
That's turkey, Sam, in every sense;

Yon turkey-buzzard on the tree:—
He's *brevet* turkey:—do you see?"

MORAL.

A Turkey has some value, Sam,
A Buzzard isn't worth a d——!

DEAD IN THE WILDERNESS.

Dead in the Wilderness! dead!
No one to know how his brave spirit fled;
Thinking of loved ones—gasping for breath!
"Oh! for a drop of cold water—or death!"

"God! can it be that thy spirit is here.
Kill me in mercy! the red flame is near!
See! how it hurries to scorch up my breath;
Oh! for a drop of cold water, or death!"

Dead in the Wilderness! dead!
Ashes the mantle that o'er him is spread.
Young—oh! so young; and so gallant and brave:
Was there no angel in heaven to save?

No one to plead for the warrior boy,
Who fought 'gainst the host that came forth to destroy;
No one to wipe from his lips the white foam,
Or hear the last word for the loved ones at home?

111

Dead in the Wilderness? no:

In the land where true warriors go,

Afar from the Wilderness, drear and unblest,

He has found 'mong the brave, his reward and his
    rest.

"LET US HAVE PEACE."

Long we struggled hand to hand,
Whilst war's tempests swept the land;
And the hopes of tyrants filled their hearts with glee,
When our country gasped for breath,
And on nerve hung life or death;
And we trembled from the mountain to the sea.

From the fight at Gaines' Mill,
To the sanguine Malvern Hill;
In the battle of the Wilderness, more dread
Than the plains where havoc drew
The red tide at Waterloo,
Did we pay the price of country, with our dead.

From Ohio's turbid wave,
To the Mississippi's grave,
Where she soothes her restless spirit in the sea;
Is the earth's green mantle spread
O'er ten thousand martyred dead,
Whom the heavens called, to make a nation free.

113

'Midst the howl of right and **wrong**;
Whether weak, or whether strong:
Still the nation bared **her bosom** to the storm,
With **a cheek that never paled**;
With **a heart that never quailed,**
And a steadfast hope **in God, to keep it warm.**

But '**tis past:**—**so let us** pray,
By the promised peace to-day,
That the North and South in harmony **may live**;
An example to the world,
Wheresoe'er our **flag's** unfurled,
Of a nation that can fight, and can forgive.

SOLDIERS' HOME, D. C., *Nov. 5th*, 1868.

FAR, FAR AWAY.

Far, far away,
In a silvery bay,
On a green little isle I was born;
I remember it well,
And how my heart fell,
When from that little isle I was torn.

That home of delight,
With its gardens so bright,
Alas! I shall never see more;
Nor the green water-willows,
That kissed all the billows,
That rolled to its beautiful shore.

How I used to sigh,
When the big ships came by,
With their sails, and their pennants so bright;
At morning to go
Where the sea-winds did blow,
And come back to my island at night.

And when from her home
The white sea-bird would roam,
And come floating on up with the tide;
How I wished for her wing,
And the power to swing
On the dark rocking wave, by her side.

Though winters of care
Have whiten'd my hair,
And plundered my cheek of its smile;
Still o'er memory's track,
'Tis a joy to look back,
To my home on that green little isle.

THE OLD MAN'S COMFORT.

I am old and gray; I am old and gray;
And my strength is failing me day by day;
But it warms my heart when the sun has gone,
And her robe of stars the night puts on,
To gaze on the glad ones who gather here,
To breathe their sweet songs on my aged ear.

They bear me back :—they bear me back—
To the field of youth, and its flowery track;
When my arm was strong, and my heart was bold,
And my first young love was not yet cold ;
And I gaze on many a smiling brow,
That sleeps in the still old church-yard now.

It wrung my heart:—oh ! it wrung my heart,
When I saw them one by one depart,
And they cost me many a tear of wo;
For my hopes then hung on the things below;
But the visions of earthly joy grow dim,
With the whitening hair, and the failing limb.

I am old and gray; I am old and gray;
But I've strength yet left me to kneel and pray;
And morning and evening I bless the power,
That woke me to light in the midnight hour;
That spared me to gaze, with an aged eye,
On a hope that can never fade nor die.

I am gliding on ; I am gliding on;
Through a quiet night, to a golden dawn;
And the merry hearts that around me play,
Are star-beams to light up my lonely way;
And oh! may the waves of life's dark sea
Deal gently with them, as they've dealt with me.

THE VAMPIRE.

Again to the busy world I come:
   'Tis damp; but not so chill
As the hollow grave—the Vampire's home—
   Where all, save the worm, is still;
Where silence sits, in her sable cowl,
And sound comes not when the tempests howl.

I walk amidst the moving crowd;
   But my footstep is not heard:
I come where voices ring aloud,
   But I murmur not a word;
For a sound from my thirsting lip would start
A thrill of fear through the stoutest heart.

Who looks on me?—well, let them stare:
   Ha! now he turns away:
Did he see the grave dew on my hair,—
   The mould that makes me gray?
Let him look again, my upas breath
Shall turn his young brow pale as death!

Yon blue-eyed girl;—behold her there:
　　Why looks her cheek so white?
Hath she drained the venom cup of care?
　　No: I knelt by her couch last night,
And drew the blood from her heart away,
That crimsoned her young brow yesterday.

She ne'er can know that sleep again,
　　Which brings the soul repose;
For a fire will burn in each shrinking vein,
　　Whenever her eyelids close:
No rest for her, till the midnight storm
Howls o'er the home of her wasted form.

She leans upon her lover's arm,
　　In her rosy vestments clad ;
He feels her tears fall fast and warm,
　　And wonders why she is sad.
He does not know how the vampire's tongue
Thirsts for the blood of the fair and young.

She goes; and I must follow where
　　Her snowy couch is spread;
The dawn will find her white corse there;
　　The living will weep the dead;
But none will know what spell hath given
The lovely form of earth, to heaven.

ON THE DEATH OF JOHN QUINCY ADAMS.

A wail of sorrow sweeps the land;
   A nation mourns her pride;
Struck down within her council halls,
   A great, good man has died;
And centuries may roll away,
Ere nature moulds again such clay.

Above life's moving multitude,
   A lofty place he had;
Though often in his "wanderings,"
   Men said that he was mad;
The "dreams" o'er which they smiled in ruth,
Time ever ripened into truth.

To shake the wisest thoughts of men,
   To him belonged the power;
For whilst they watched the dial hand,
   He looked beyond the hour;
Prompted by truth's unerring law,
He pointed, and the nation saw.

Hale as the morn,—for threescore years
  He walked the earth, and when
At last pale palsy snatched his arm,
  Youth still sat on his pen;
And smiling called the muses there
  To warble for the young and fair.

"This is the last of earth;" strange words
  To fill life's latest sigh.
Few ever lived, as he did live,
   To die as he did die:
  "I am content," the old man said;
  Then to the victor, bowed his head.

ANOTHER YEAR.

"I heard an old man's dying sigh,
  And an infant's idle laughter;
And the old year went with a moaning by,
  And the new came dancing after."

Another year:—and gray-beard Time
  Is hurrying onward still;
He is weaving the changes of tide and clime,
And ringing the bells with a holiday chime,
  That echoes from every hill.

Through manhood's breast what sorrows pour,
  Musing on things that have passed
Down life's rapid river, to rise no more;
The friends who have glided away from its shore,
  Since the holiday bells rang last!

Death touched the girl of the laughing eye,
  And pale grew her cheek and brow,
He smiled at the youth as he hurried by;
Then left him alone, to linger and die,
  Like an autumn leaf on the bough.

123

We mourn the buried with a tear;
　Why not for the living weep:—
The young, the blooming; another year,
Ah! who can tell,—will *they* be here,
　With their joys so wild and deep?

"Sister!" I heard a brother say,
　With a laugh of boyish pride,
"To-morrow will be a holiday;
I will deck your brow with garlands gay,
　I have plucked by the mountain side.

"And you shall join the festive ring,
　And sport the merriest there:
So happily will we dance and sing,
Whilst joy as fresh in your heart will spring
　As the leaves that deck your hair."

Ah! for that youth! the morrow came,
　And wafted his pride away:
That sister's eye hath lost its flame;
Where yon willow sweeps we read her name,
　O'er the cold, dark home of clay.

Alas! that man, his house of joy
　Should build upon the sand:
Too soon the fabric doth Time destroy;
For life to him is an idle toy
　In a child's destructive hand.

But soft! 'tis an old man's dying sigh;
  Bring forth the pall and the bier;
Quick! quick! for the child of the laughing eye
And the rosy cheek is drawing nigh:
  He must not see him here.

GIVE US RAIN.

The rivers are shallow,—the fountains are dry,—
 The leaf of the lily is withered and brown;
Yet day after day, from a cloudless sky,
 Pour the burning rays till the sun goes down.

" No sign of rain !" is the greeting word,
 When the mist to the morning ray is given;
" What a lovely sky !" at eve is heard,
 " Not a single cloud on the face of heaven."

The breeze is hot as it loiters by,—
 And the cottager's cheek is pale and worn;
He has looked too long, with an aching eye,
 On the drooping leaves of his silking corn.

The child that wakes to the morning light
 Knows not why its mother's brow is sad:
She has wept and prayed through the livelong night
 O'er her parching fields, in the moonlight clad.

The girl goes **forth in the morning hour,**
   To cull, for her golden **hair, a wreath;**
But she sees no dew upon the **flower,**
   Nor the withered grass her feet beneath.

God, send us rain!—Let thy children see
   Thy smiling face, in the gathering cloud;
All nature thirsting, turns to thee,—
   And earth is ceasing to be proud.

OH! STRANGE IS DEATH.

Oh! strange is death; and fearfully
  Its shadow falls upon the heart,
When friends around stand tearfully,
  To watch the struggling soul depart.
Oh! strange is death; but stranger still
  The ways of the Almighty God,
When desolation marks His will,
  And hearts are breaking at His nod.

I see a lovely child at prayer,
  Her little hands upon her breast;
And she has come to worship where
  A sister's form is laid at rest:
When the evening breeze is blowing,
  When the earth is bright and glad,
Why, oh! why should tears be flowing;
  Why should that young heart be sad?

Oh! strange is death; but stranger still
  The ways of the Almighty God,
When desolation marks His will,
  And hearts are breaking at His nod.

129

I see an aged father's form,
  Low bending o'er his dying child;
And fearful as the bursting storm
  Is his wailing, deep and wild.
"Father! father! hear my prayer;
Hear me, God, in my despair;
We know Thou wilt her sins forgive:
But smile, oh! smile, and let her live."

Man's prayer is vain whilst angels wait:
Father, thy home is desolate.

A laugh rings in the busy street;
  Some merry heart is passing by:
It dreams not of the winding sheet:—
Trip on,—trip on, with dancing feet;
  Ne'er think that happy youth can die.

Oh! strange is death; but stranger still
  The ways of the Almighty God,
Whose wisdom shines upon the hill,
  Where mortal foot hath never trod.

THE POET'S DEATH-BED.

Darkness in the lone chamber of the dead!
Light for the dying!   Draw the curtain back,
And let the sun shine in upon my bed.

There,—there:—'tis kind:—I would not breathe my
    last
Mantled in darkness,—dying like the worm:
No,—give my spirit light,—and let me gaze
Once more on nature, through these dying eyes;
And breathe my farewell to the golden hills,
The stream, the lake, the forest; things for which
Dark years have failed to lessen my young love.

All else that I have worshipped since my youth,
Died,—or was false:—I loved the sparkling eye,
And basked beneath its light but for a day,
And it grew dim: I sought the laureled hill,
The hill whereon Fame's towering temple stands;
Upon whose turrets falls, in light from heaven,
The broad, bright blaze of science; but my heart
broke in its mighty reachings; and I fell,—

Down,—down so far, Ambition for a while
Withheld her light; and darkness o'er my soul
Hung, like the midnight pall that wraps the world.

Life! I have walked thy paths,—and learned them
  well:
And they are solitary,—joy is not,—
And hope is but an idle, lying hand,
That points the soul to that it cannot reach;
Strewing the way with flowers,—then with thorns,—
And leads the fool to madness and to death.

Close not the curtain! Let the breeze come in
And toss my locks about, as it was wont
In days gone by, upon the mountain side.

I long to feel the struggle of the soul,
And learn if there be agony in Death;
For I have deemed the dissolution joy.

He comes!—he comes! his hand is on my heart:
How coldly swept that breeze across my brow!

Another, and another;—colder still;
Dark!—dark! Methinks the sun is in eclipse,
Sure, Night hath not a shadow like to this.
But see! what star is that?—it fades; 'tis gone:
Now bright again:—farewell! how sweet,—farewell!

THINKING—THINKING, TILL DAYLIGHT IS GONE.

Thinking—thinking, till daylight is gone;
Dreaming—dreaming through darkness till dawn:
And so does the busy machine work on:—
                    Man and his brain.
How will it,—when will it,—where will it stop ?
God pours his oil on it, drop by drop,
                    And all its work is vain.

Vain, to the eyes that cannot see;
Vain, mortal worm, to you and me;
                    But He knows all.

And so, when our earthly woof is spun,
And the wheels of life have ceased to run,
And we say good-night! to the stars and the sun,
                    May He not call:—

He who came forth to ransom men;
To win them back to God again;
Call to his Father in that hour,

Rich in his mercy and his power;
And plead forgiveness for the past
For all who have sinned,—the first,—the last
Since Adam's fall.

I WEEP THE SUMMER COME AGAIN.

I weep the summer come **again**;
The hillside with its waving grain;
The robin sipping at the spring;
The flutter of the blue-bird's wing;
The clover blossom peeping through
The shining nest of leaf **and** dew.
I weep, because when summer-time
Last smiling came, my humble **rhyme**
Was spun for one that's gone before;
To walk beyond the shining shore,
The daisy banks for evermore.

I weep the summer come again;
The fragrant breeze o'er hill and plain.
The rill, long bound in winter's lock,
Now leaps the cliff, from rock to rock;
The bright cascade, that all day long
Sings **to** the woods its sylvan song.

Down in the glen where last we met,
Methinks I hear her sweet voice yet;
But oh! 'tis such a world of pain,
To know, and feel, that ne'er again,
When summer comes with leaf and flower,
Our steps will seek that rosy bower
Where we were wont, 'midst songs of birds,
To breathe love tales, in whispered words.

I weep the summer come again:
Yet why, when tears are all in vain,
Should mine not be a joyous heart?
For we are not so far apart;—
A little gauzy veil between
What soon will be, and what has been;
When Time shall draw that veil aside,
Ah! then, the joyful summer-tide
Of sun and flowers, that nevermore
Will leave us on lone winter's shore,
But dwell with us for evermore.

"GRIN AND BEAR IT."

If your true love cast you by,
   And in grief you've none to share it;
Show that grief to no man's eye,—
Or woman's either:—"ne'er say die;"
   But "grin and bear it."

If, in trouble, friends depart—
   And they'll do so, you may swear it—
Smile,—look jolly,—play your part,
Though their falseness crush your heart;
   And "grin and bear it."

Nothing's ever gained by sighs,—
   Or frowns:—Your best smile ever wear it;
Conceal your wounds from others' eyes;
And swell out,—and look twice your size,
   And "grin and bear it."

If Shylocks "catch you on the hip,"
   Seize not your hair to rend and tear it;
But "keep a good stiff upper lip;"
At Fortune smile, and "let her rip!"
   "And grin and bear it"

SITTING IN THE LONELY WILDWOOD.

Sitting in the lonely wildwood,
   Whilst I watched the twilight die,
Stole upon me dreams of childhood,
   One by one, like stars on high.
Dreaming,—dreaming, of the olden
   Time when days went dancing by;
Watching,—weeping o'er the golden
   Memories that cannot die:
Like the winds o'er harpstrings sighing,
Came that voice so low and dying.

" Sister, art thou very certain;
   Hast thou counted well the hours?
Draw aside the darkening curtain,
   Let me gaze upon the flowers.
Bring me buds from 'mong the roses,
   Weave them, sister, in my hair:
He will come ere daylight closes,
   And his lips will press them there."

" Weeping, sister,—ever weeping:
    Why these tears upon my brow ?
Did I talk of him whilst sleeping?
    I did dream of him—but now:—
All the summer flowers were blowing,
    And such joy my spirit wore;
For I thought that he was coming,
    He that can come nevermore."

"Sing to me,—how once a maiden,
    When death stole her love away;
Though her heart was heavy laden,
    Watched his coming, day by day.
How she sat beneath the willows,
    Weaving flowerets for her hair;
Till she sought him 'neath the billows,
    Hoping still to find him there.

"Sing to me! nay, cease thy sorrow;
    Thou shouldst be all smiles to-night;
We'll be wedded on the morrow,
    At the golden gates of light."

DECORATION DAY.

What grave is this?—No mourner here,
To strew a flower, or shed a tear?

"'Tis Brown's," a one-armed soldier said;
"They've overlooked him 'mong the dead;
There are so many scattered here.
Brown's grave:—I saw him when he fell;
  It was not on a day like this;
Above,—before,—around us,—hell!
  Now all is sunshine, peace and bliss."

And then the empty sleeve was spread,
To drink the tear the soldier shed.

"God rest his soul!"—and so prayed I;
  And then I thought, if from the skies
Brown's soul could look through that bright day,
  The gladdest thing beneath his eyes,
Would be that comrade with his say—
         "God rest his soul!"

THE BAYONET BOYS.

[Written impromptu, and sung at a collation given to the Louisiana Delegation, at Matamoras, Mexico, appointed to present the thanks of Louisiana to General Taylor and his Army.]

Come, fill up your glasses,—the night hurries on;
And I'll give you a song ere this bottle is gone;
And the chorus shall be, when the cork has been
   drawn,
   Huzza for brave **Zack, and his Bayonet Boys**!

By the green Palo Alto we first met the foe,
Where we taught him the trick of fight hard and lie
   low;
And convinced him that there was more metal than
   show,
   In General Zack, and his Bayonet Boys.

The noon it was sultry,—the balls flew so hot,
They made dodging a science in that busy spot;
And the copper they threw will not soon be forgot
   By General Zack, and his **Bayonet Boys**.

140

Sublime to all gazers, their show and their art;
But sublime and ridiculous aren't far apart;
Soon the joke grew so fat that we took it to heart,
    And they heard from brave Zack, and his Bayonet
        Boys !

A voice from our Ringgold, whose body lies low,
Where the prairie grass waves, and the wild flowers
      grow,
Was a prelude of death to full many a foe,
    Who fell before Zack, and his Bayonet Boys.

Oh! long may the wild flower grow on the grave
Of the hero who falls 'midst the tug of the brave;
And long may remembrance his valor engrave
    On the hearts of Old Zack, and his Bayonet Boys.

But pass round the bowl, and let Mexico sweat
O'er the rout and defeat she will not soon forget:
If she does, there's more food for remembrance "to
    let,"
    By inquiring of Zack, and his Bayonet Boys.

LET US FILL FOR THE HOPE TO-MORROW.

[Written the night before Palo Alto.]

From the sunny South,—from the North land drear,
  With our starry flag above us;
At our country's call, we are gathered here,
  To fight for the hearts that love us.
The eye of a nation, bold and free,
  Grows bright, as it watches o'er us;
And we own no heart would bend the knee
  To the proudest foe before us.

The fiends of the ocean held their wrath,
  As our barks o'er the waves came leaping;
And the steady trade-winds smoothed our path
  On the deep, whilst the storms were sleeping:
All strong of arm, and firm of heart,
  We now hold the Texan Border;
And crave one fight, before we part,
  Just to keep our Boys in order.

But since we cannot fight to-day,
   Let's fill for the hope to-morrow;
And pledge to the true hearts, far away,
   Whom our absence fills with sorrow;
And if in fight our blood we spill,
   'Tis a happy consolation,
To know for us some eye will fill,
   Who died for the " annexation."

ARLINGTON.

How still the Army sleeps to-night,
Beneath the pale moon's trembling light;
No dreaming of the morrow's fight;
            The victory's won.
The silent stars their vigils keep;
No flames that flash from plain or steep
Can wake them from their quiet sleep;
            Their work is done.

O'er dewy grass no sentry's tread;
The green leaves whisper overhead
A lowly requiem for the dead,
            Who live in fame.
Whilst Freedom breathes, what hand shall dare
Disturb them in their slumber there?
Who lives, so infamous, to share
            Such deed of shame?

Whilst low winds sigh,—whilst tempests roar,
Beneath these shades for evermore,
Where broad Potomac laves the shore,
            Thy beds shall be.

As freemen's hearts grow pure and strong,
And men forget imagined wrong,
Thousands above these graves will throng,
    To honor thee.

Oh! 'twas a great and glorious fight;
Fierce for the wrong,—fierce for the right;
But now sweet Peace her mantle bright
    Hath spread o'er all.
Calmly we sit above the slain,
With mingled thoughts of joy and pain,
Marveling if e'er this land again
    Such wo befall.

THE LIMERICK BOY.

May the devil take the Sergeant, and his circumvent-
    ing crew,
Who seduced me to the rendezvous, and dressed me
    up in blue;
Who measured me, and told me I was just the boy to
    win
The epaulettes in half a year, if I would just go in.
                          Bad luck to them!

They marched me to the depot,—a charming little
    isle,
Just off the city of New York,—about an Irish mile;
Where, when I saw the banners wave and heard the
    music play,
I thought myself a fairy boy, just landed from the bay.
                           Bad luck to it!

If Mary Kelly could have seen the Limerick boy that
    morn,
As he swaggered through the sally-port, with head
    and whiskers shorn,

With foot so light, **and eye** so bright, she would have
  rued the day
She jilted him, **and drove him from Ould** Ireland
  away.

> **Bad** luck to her!

But a change came o'er my spirit before another
  morn,
When they shoved **me on a** transport, bound **for**
  "Eden"—"in a horn;"
Then hadn't I the golden dream of hammocks, swamps,
  and **brakes,**
A soldiering **in** Florida,—'mong centipedes and snakes?

> Bad luck to **it!**

If I ever catch that Sergeant,—the insinuating scamp,
There'll be music in the quarters,—there'll be mutiny
  in **camp;**
For I'll **lie for him as** surely as my name is Paddy Bly,
And I'll have **a little** settlement, or **know** the reason
  why.

> Bad luck to him!

A DRAMATIC SKETCH.

Scene—A Wood. Neenah resting on a bank, her child sleeping by her side.

NEENAH. Haste!—haste, thou tardy moon!
Leap like a maiden's glance to her love star;
And throw thy broad beams on yon broken pine.
'Tis joy to sit beside the forest stream,
And watch thy coming, when his voice is near;
To mingle with the sighing winds,—and breathe
On Neenah's wakeful ear the joyous words,—
"I love thee!"—but when he is far away,
The night creeps sadly, and the dews that fall
Seem tears from joyless eyes that weep for Neenah.
He bade me watch yon lightning-shattered bough;
And told me, when the moonbeam rested there,
To listen for his foot-fall by the stream.
My eyes are pained with watching;—will he come?
Tardy moon!—weary, weary Neenah.

(Sleeps.)

Enter Halaka, as from hunting; he stops, leans upon his bow, and gazes for a time, silently, upon the sleepers.

HALAKA. My timid doe! and her young fawn;
Sleep ye so soundly, when the wolves are near?
Methinks it were a golden season now,

To send their free hearts to the spirit land,
Ere they do wake to slavery and chains.
The storm is coming:—I have watched it long,
Gathering in might above our forest homes;
'Twill burst!—and blood will follow,—even now
The white man's plume is waving 'neath our pines;
And fast before the gleam of burnished arms,
Fly the affrighted tenants of the wild.
The stag no longer shuns the red man's path;
His eye is dazzled by a stranger foe;
And from the hammock drear, the black wolf's cry
Swells like a warning, on the midnight air.
A silent spirit floats above our homes,
That dares not speak, yet stirs all hearts to conflict.

(*Neenah awakes.*)

NEENAH. Halaka, I am glad thou art returned:
I watched for thee with anxious heart,—and long;
But o'er my head the green leaves sang so low,
They wooed me to the land of crazy thought;
And I did dream of battle and of blood;
And 'midst the strife, where shouts went wildest up
Of victory and vengeance, I did see
Thine eagle plume wave high above the host;
And ever where thy form was seen, a child,—
The image of our boy, but decked with wings,—

Hung o'er it:—and its tiny shout did seem
To stir thy heart to madness,—why is this?
My husband! there is lightning in thine eyes,
And on thy brow sits darkness,—do the words
Of idle Neenah anger thee? why, then,
She'll speak no more.

    HALAKA. Go on!

        NEENAH. I would not have thee sad.

            HALAKA. Go on! the dream!

    NEENAH. Why, this was all the dream.

    HALAKA. All?—all?—ha! ha!—I'll tell thee of a
            dream—
A waking dream:—there's music in it,—hark!
Thou know'st the Uchee's wigwam,—where it stood
Beneath the tall palms, by the Miccos lake;
A happy home for the old white-haired sire,
Whom often thou hast seen, at dawn of day,
Leading his brawny children in the chase;
Or teaching them to guide the light canoe
Across the lake when winds and waves were high.
I had been hunting by Kahiwa stream,
And wending homeward, saw, above the palms,
A cloud of smoke that dimmed the eye of day,
And heard, upon the breeze that bore it on,

The wild and fearful shouts of frantic men.
Nearing the lake with hasty step, I saw
The good old Uchee's wigwam wrap'd in flames.
I saw the old man raise his withered arm,
To strike one blow for vengeance; but it fell,
Palsied forever,—and his spirit fled,
On the same breeze that bore the white man's laugh
Up to the God he worships.   Ask'st thou now,
Why in Halaka's eye the lightning gleams?

SONG OF THE SHAVE.

(A PARODY.)

"For razors cut as well as knives."—OLD SONG.

Shave! shave! shave!
  Is the song of the frontier line:
Lather, and pull, and scrape,
  Till your eyes are swimming in brine.
Razor, and soap, and brush;
  Brush, and razor, and soap;
If down on your chin, your pride has been,
  It must slope,—slope,—slope.

Whip, and bridle, and spur;
  Bridle, and spur, and whip:
By the foaming steed does the order speed
  To Bomford, and Monty, and Rip;
And away to the Wichita,
  It flies on the winds like chaff:
Be serious, boys,—and don't "ha! ha!"
  'Tis vulgar to laugh,—laugh.

152

Red, and sable, and gray;
   Sable, and gray, and red:
Each whiskered cheek must be sickled sleek,
   At the sound of the courser's tread.
Toothache, and tic douloureux,
   Coughs, and fevers, and chills;
Doctors have work to do,—
   With their pills, squills, **pills.**

Simple cerate and salve,
   For the lips that are cracked **and sore**;
And flannel bands for the throats
   That will revel in beards **no** more.
Muffle your chins, when the wind begins
   To sweep from its icy **land**;
When it cuts the hide, on the prairies **wide,**
   Where the scattered post-oaks stand.

Jones, **and** Crawford, **and** Brooke;
   Brooke, and Crawford, and Jones;
Send on, if you can, the Razor Strap Man,
   With his hones,—hones,—hones;
And send us some Sheffield **blades,**
   With backs from the silver mine;
For it frets our lives, when barlow-knives
   Come forth in the shaving line.

Shave! shave! shave!
  Lather, and brush, and smear!
Lather and brush, and cut with a rush,
  Is the song of the new frontier.

[10] " HOUGH!"

Lonely by the camp-fire dreaming,
Whilst the stars are o'er me beaming,
Memory and thought come streaming,
    Rainbow-like, across my brow.
Scenes that fate cannot deny me,
Float upon the night-winds by me,
Whilst dark cares forgotten fly me;
    And in dreams, I drink to "hough!"
"Hough!" boys, "hough!"—"hough!" boys, "hough!"
Drink beneath the tall palmetto,

                  " Hough!"

Soldier boys should never borrow
Idle troubles for the morrow;
Time enough, when comes the sorrow,
    'Neath its heavy weight to bow.
Then, whilst stars are shining o'er us,
Let not darker skies before us
In our dreams wake bitter chorus,
    Banishing the toast of "hough!"
"Hough!" boys, "hough!"—"hough!" boys, "hough!"
Underneath the green palmetto, "hough!"

Pressing here my mossy pillow,
Forms that moulder 'neath the willow,—
Forms that sleep beneath the billow,
    Flit and frolic 'round me now,
Banishing all thought of mourning;
All my dreams with joy adorning;
May they tarry till the morning,
    Ere they breathe their parting "hough!"
"Hough!" boys, "hough!"—"hough!" boys, "hough!"
Let the soldier's toast be, ever, "hough!"

NOTES.

PAGE 13.

[1]*The Express Rider.*

The gallantry, energy, and daring displayed by those who, during the Florida war, followed the wild business of riding express from post to post, through those lonely and dangerous wildernesses, has, perhaps, never been surpassed in ancient or in modern times. On the principal roads or trails over which they held their rapid course, there is scarcely a hammock, or place for ambush, which has not rung to the triumphant song of the red savage, over his bleeding victim; or to the vindictive yell which followed the flying adventurer, when the erring rifle, or the erring hand, failed to accomplish its bloody work. Yet, strange to say, urged either by that spirit of adventure which a life in the wilderness is so apt to engender, or for the sake of notoriety among their comrades, volunteers, from the ranks of the Army, were ever to be found, ready and anxious for the dangerous service.

[2]*And the tall pine shadow is over us cast.*

The danger was confined to the swamps and hammocks; in the pines there was safety.

PAGE 14.

[3] *When thy wild eye tells me the foe is near.*

Any one at all familiar with border life in the Indian country, knows that the horse is the best sentinel or advance guard he can have,—and that he never fails, by day or night, to give warning of approaching danger.

PAGE 27.

[4] *The Chained Seminole.*

Coacooche, or Wild-Cat, was a chief of great daring and celebrity in the Seminole war. After more than three years of successful combat with those whom he deemed the enemies of his race, and the unlawful invaders of his soil, he was seized, with his brother, and thirteen warriors, whilst on a visit to Fort Pierce, and thus separated from his wife and child. He was placed in irons, and on board of a vessel launched upon the broad waters, to find a home, he knew not, nor he cared not, whither:—to quote his own language : "It is plain that, die where I may, the grass above my head will bend beneath the tread of the white man." He was young and handsome,— when unruffled, gentle as a woman,—when aroused to anger terrible as a demon,—and his quick wit and eloquence in the council will long be remembered by those who have blushed to hear him speak the red man's wrongs.

[5] *I think upon my father's* **grave.**

King Philip died at sea, a prisoner.

> ⁶*But yesterday,* **and I** *could claim*
> *The eagle feather for my brow.*

The eagle feather, the insignia of highest **rank among the** Seminole tribes.

PAGE 41.

> ⁷*I think of* **my** *wife and child.*

Written on the Gulf of Mexico, at the outbreak of the Mexican **war, when families were** broken up, and sailing in **different directions.**

PAGE 78.

> ⁸*Shamed not her father's pride.*

This line has allusion **to** tears, which even from the soft eye **of woman are** deemed disgraceful among the Indian tribes of the **North.**

PAGE 103.

> ⁹*I'm standing by thy dwelling.*

Lt. J. E. Blake, Engineer Corps, killed at Palo Alto.

PAGE 155.

> ¹⁰*"Hough!"*

An army sentiment, well understood **in the** Florida war,—but although uttered as a toast, generally, throughout the army at **the** present time, there are but few who know its origin. Coacooche, **or** Wild-Cat, the distinguished Seminole chief, at the time of his surrender at Camp Cummins, Florida, observing that **the officers used certain** expressions, such as "here's luck!"

"the old grudge!" etc., before drinking, asked Gofer John, a negro interpreter, what they said. John was puzzled; but finally explained by saying, "It means how d'ye do!" whereupon the chief, with great dignity, lifted his cup, and elevating it above his head, exclaimed in a deep, guttural, and triumphant voice, *"Hough !"*

The word was at once adopted by the officers of the 8th Infantry and 2d Dragoons, and as a sentiment spread rapidly throughout the whole Army.

www.ingramcontent.com/pod-product-compliance
Lightning Source LLC
Chambersburg PA
CBHW020014030726
47500CB00002B/579